Chrissy Derbyshire is a writer, folklorist and storyteller living in Cardiff. She has told her stories at firesides, in noisy pubs and in festival marquees to an unsought backdrop of shamanic drumming. Her essays have been published in *Labyrinth* and *The Raconteur*, among others, and one of her stories was recently published in *The Wish Dog: Haunting Tales from Welsh Women Writers*.

Mysteries

Chrissy Derbyshire

AWEN

Stroud

First published in 2008 by Awen Publications

This second (expanded) edition published by Awen Publications 2018
12 Belle Vue Close, Stroud GL5 1ND, England
www.awenpublications.co.uk

Front cover image by Tom Brown
Copyright © 2016 Tom Brown

Cover design: Kirsty Hartsiotis
Editing: Anthony Nanson
Proofreading: Richard Selby

ISBN 978-1-906900-45-8

To Anwen Aurora,

who was not called Bridey in the end

CONTENTS

FOREWORD

Mythology is not a lie, mythology is poetry, it is meta-
phorical. It has been well said that mythology is the penultimate truth – penultimate because the ultimate cannot be put into words. It is beyond words. Beyond images, beyond that bounding rim of the Buddhist Wheel of
Becoming. Mythology pitches the mind beyond that rim,
to what can be known but not told.

Joseph Campbell, *The Power of Myth*

When we speak of mythology, the mind immediately conjures
up images of ancient Greece and its petty, passionate deities, of
the green gods of the British Isles as they once were, of the
mysteries found in the red earth of Australia and the many-
armed devas of India. We think of fantastic stories that are distant and dead, and people whose names we will never know.
We do not place ourselves in that world, for it is not ours.
Chrissy Derbyshire knows differently, and with *Mysteries*, her
first collection, published originally in 2008, she offers us a way
to claim a place in myth as partakers of story.

Every story, whether it is told by mothers to the children on
their knees or by priests to ecstatic worshipers, takes place in
the mode of mythology. It presents a journey and the happen-
ings along its way, and we, the readers, are invited to identify
with each character as they arrive. Stories serve a great number
of purposes, that of entertainment being ubiquitous, but the
best stories create landscapes that the reader can internalise,
using them to build inner worlds in which they can undertake

the most divine journey of individuation, awakening and growth.

Myths and fairy tales inform and enrich our inner landscapes and feed our souls, guiding us to greater self-awareness and awareness of others. We hear them as some of the earliest stories we learn, passed down to us in an oral and written tradition from our parents, who had them passed to them in the same way. When we tell stories and consume them, we step into that rich stream of story and become part of it. We are offered a chance to own each story and subtly direct its flow. For most of us, this is done with little awareness. But Chrissy's work in *Mysteries* builds consciously on these stories, claims them and directs them into new, fresh streams, where they take on life of their own. She walks on the same roads as Angela Carter and Neil Gaiman, and her characters are just two in number: the quintessential Everyman and Everywoman. At the same time, her work is deeply personal and charts the course of her own growing self during those formative, youthful years of her twenties. Yet the stories and poems in *Mysteries* reflect themes, challenges and ideas that almost all of us discover in our own journeys. It is not just Chrissy's poor, frightening Siren who longs for somebody who will have the courage to accept her for who she is rather than imagining a perfect version of her, but us too. We have all undergone, or can hope to do so, a sort of preparation in readiness for our own deaths, learning to accept our mortality as Chrissy does in 'My Grave'. We have all been Ashling from 'The Mysteries', finding our way in fear and sorrow to a liminal place and there being offered a choice that will decide our next path. Whether Ashling chooses to stay in the Underworld with Persephone and her half-people, I think, will differ from reader to reader.

All of the pieces in *Mysteries* are entertaining. But they also speak twice. Each one has layers of meaning that touch on the ultimate that cannot be put into words and speak to our inner landscapes that are so full of desire for meaning. Chrissy's journey, elaborately retold in the arena of mythology, is our own journey, and the words contained herein could have come from our own hearts and mouths. Chrissy, stepping into the role of bard – that most sacred duty of spokesman for the people and the gods – has given us the symbols and signposts of our lives and wrapped them up in beautiful, powerful words. We are truly blessed.

Kim Huggens

INTRODUCTION

Mystery is an unknown, secret or hidden thing, a thing that cannot be explained. It is strangeness itself. By one definition it is a weird or puzzling story, by another a thing made known by divine revelation. I chose the title 'Mysteries' for this collection because each piece tells of something strange, wonderful, terrible, inexplicable and divine. Yet, perhaps unexpectedly, each piece is also rooted in the everyday. Strange things happen in the lives of normal people. Fabulous beasts dream human dreams. And the gods, the gods are everywhere.

The title 'Mysteries' also echoes one of the stories in this collection. 'The Mysteries' is so called because of its link to the Eleusinian Mysteries: the ancient initiation rites of the cult of Demeter and Persephone at Eleusis in Greece. Persephone, maiden Goddess of Spring, was picking flowers when Hades, her uncle and Lord of Death, abducted her and dragged her down to the Underworld. In her distress at her daughter's disappearance, Demeter, Goddess of the Harvest, neglected herself and the world. As she mourned, the world became barren. Finally she discovered the truth of Persephone's abduction and entered the Underworld to claim her daughter back. But Demeter was too late: Persephone had already eaten three pomegranate seeds, each representing a month ruling as Queen of Death in the Underworld. And so, each year, she descends to the Underworld for three months, leaving her mother in mourning and the Earth barren. This is what we call 'winter'.

It is not essential to read these stories and poems in the order in which they are presented. Taken alone, each represents a different moment in time, a different encapsulation of emotions, a different portion of that Otherworld which superimposes upon our own. Yet, taken together, they are intended to mirror the strange and often disturbing descent into the Underworld, and the emergence, reborn, into the light of mundane reality. These stories and poems have taken me to strange places. I hope they have the same effect – or an entirely different effect – on you.

Chrissy Derbyshire
Cardiff, Lammas 2008

HARP

Old shapeshifting thing,
You still stand there singing my words,
Shaped rather like
This poem that describes you.
Now old as the dust floor,
Creaking from within – sounds of an ancient wood –
With thick strings loose and curled
Like spirals to the centre
That is, in the end, a tomb.
All flesh there has turned to dust
Many years beyond memory.
The stone has faded, fallen,
Been covered with earth and forgotten,
But pluck the timeworn strings
And some echoes remain.
Now she is pale as a green youth,
Trembling with the flowers of first poetry,
Tied with merry ribbons
And singing out birdsong in gardens.
Then I like to dip her in the well
And pull her out laughing
As the rivulets run down her may-scented body.
It harms her not –
Just means that she can play water music.
More often than not, she does.
She is a conch shell strung with the hair of sirens.
She sounds with the sound of otherworldly cries,

Of fishes leaping into pools
And of the mighty storm.
O storm-tossed singer!
I hold her like a sailor shipwrecked
When after months on a barren island
This harp washes on to my shore.
Though she makes no sound,
This driftwood skeleton,
Her voice swallowed by the sea,
Still I will weep with joy,
Run my hand over no strings
And play emptiness music to the stars.

THE MYSTERIES

Ashling presses forward in torn dress and muddy boots.

Never again, she tells herself.

No more.

It had been just another night in the bright, dark place. Just another ghastly fumble under the pulsing strobe. Just another sickening tangle with another unlikely lover. The last. Now she ran for her life through the sheet rain and ghosts of trees. Flashback images poured from her shorted mind to project themselves on the rain-wall.

Last night and too many nights before. Pills and vomiting, too-bright lights and kisses that taste like dust. So many parties. So few conversations.

She hated it. But if she didn't go …

A moan of wind and rain lifted Ashling's hair as she ran. This might have been fun, the Halloween Frightfest. October 31st; deserted house in the woods; come as a dead person – she had come in her own clothes, which everyone agreed was really cool; elite few only. She had been among the elite. A rare honour. Her popularity must have increased: her plan had been a success. Yet more images swept from her, out on to the night.

Eleven years old, a girl with unkempt brown hair and wide, ecstatic eyes reads The Magicians *at her desk. It flies out of her hands. She looks up to see a pretty, sharp-faced girl in gold earrings flicking roughly through it.*

'God!' she spits. 'She's a witch! Angela! Hey Angela! Everyone! Come and see, Ashling's a witch!' She reads with relish to the gathered crowd:

'Lord of evil, thou who dost reward our sins and heinous ...' this word mispronounced *'... and heinous vices, Satan, it is thou whom we adore ...'*

The class laughs horribly.

'It's just a story!' shouts Ashling over the snorts and brays. 'That's just ... it's just a conversation! It's out of context! Listen! How it starts ... "They were in a cab jolting along the Rue de Vaugirard." It's just a ...'

'Witch! Witch! Witch! Witch! Witch!'

Ashling feels a tightening around the throat as torn pages float out of the window on to the newly cut grass.

The projection faded. What a choice she had. To be her or to be them. The Frightfest, which should have been at least a little exciting, had been the same as every night preceding it. Another day in the time-loop: same night, different setting. The lights and the darkness. Writhing bodies, this time made up like corpses. Corpse entwined with corpse. How many corpses can I snog in one night? Corpses throwing up in the hall. Corpses with their make-up running, crying on the stairs.

She was far enough away now, although the heavy beat still pulsed in her head. Still running, she screamed, loud and long. 'I'm Ashling!' she shouted over the rain and wind. 'Ashling! Ashling! I'm Ashling ...'

She fell. The ground was soft, scratchy and wet under her hands and knees. 'I'm Ashling,' she said quietly. 'I'm Ashling ... what are you?'

She was addressing a large mound of earth covered in sodden autumn leaves. There was a hole in it – almost a cave – quite large enough for a small person to crawl through. She wiped the rain and tears out of her eyes. Why not? Being buried alive would be no more tedious than this. It could be a refreshing change. So long since I've had an adventure.

Ashling crawled into the hole. It smelled of earth and spices, of decay, and of the musk of animals. On and on she crawled, surprised that it reached so far underground. She did not know

4

of an animal that would make such a hole for itself. A badger, maybe? But after she had crawled for some time the space seemed to expand until it was large enough to comfortably walk.

Ashling's heart pounded. It was moist, musty and dark, but not unpleasantly so. Suddenly she stopped. She strained her eyes at a point somewhere in the distance. She was sure she had seen, just for a moment, a flickering light. Yes, there it was again, brief and dim, but undeniably real. She began to walk again.

The light she had seen belonged to a primitive-looking sconce, a flaming torch inserted into a hole in the wall. As she walked on, more sconces appeared on either side of the tunnel. Then she stopped. The tunnel ended as abruptly as it had begun. Ashling was faced with a wall of earth, rich and moist and alive with roots. She felt bereft. Petulantly she pounded the wall, and was surprised when it gave a little under her fists. She hit it some more. A small hole formed.

Now Ashling dug with a fierce fervour. In her black cocktail dress, shredded by branches and thorns in the wood, she scrabbled like a burrowing creature, all claws and sleek fur and blind, black eyes. She was still half-blinded with her zeal to dig when strong hands clasped her arms and pulled her bodily through the hole she had made.

It took some time to adjust to the new light, and to the new reality she had penetrated. The room was huge and every sound vibrated through the walls' tender roots. Like the earthen corridor, the walls were lined with sconces, but that was by far the least surprising thing. For a sumptuous tune that was not a tune chimed through the air, and the hall was filled with people. Or nearly-people. Some were partly invisible. Some were skeletal, retaining the merest suggestion of flesh. Some looked badly drawn, scribbled by someone who knew what people ought to look like only in theory. Some declared their presence only by preserving the play of light which fell on non-existent skin. All were masked. All were dancing.

Dazed and mystified, yet somehow not scared, Ashling now looked up into the face – the mask – of the one who had lifted her through the hole. Waist-length pale red hair surrounded a white mask that entirely covered the figure's face. On one side a single black tear, stretched slightly as though by Dali, streaked down the bone-white surface. The figure wore a simple white gown. A woman, no more than a small, delicate-boned woman, yet she had lifted Ashling like a flower. Ashling noticed that the woman was not, like her companions, incomplete or shadowy. Indeed, she herself felt foggy and indistinct in comparison. This woman was, somehow, more real, more actual, more there than anything she had ever seen.

'Ashling,' a voice began, 'you have come to join us.'

Ashling stared around for the source of the voice, but soon realised it had emerged from the red and white lady standing before her. Silly, really. She had expected the mask's lips to move.

'I came here by accident,' answered Ashling, though she was not sure whether the woman expected an answer. If she answered, it implied a question, and she suspected – with a dull ache of portent – that what she had heard was no question.

'Besides,' she said, 'how do you know who I am?'

There was a slow pause. 'It is my business to know who enters my domain. It is my lot to know. I … know …'

Ashling waited for several seconds to hear what the woman knew, but apparently she had forgotten – or the sentence was already completed. She decided to change the subject.

'These people … they're …?'

'Dead,' said the masked woman.

'But they're dancing.'

'I am often abroad in the Middle World. I pick up these customs and pass them on.'

'But a masquerade? Isn't that … well, isn't it rather an old-fashioned custom … I mean, these days?'

'I pass on that which it pleases me to pass on.'

The soft tones had not changed, but at this Ashling knew, as she knew she was alive, that she must ask no more.

'Come,' said the woman. 'Let us dance.'

Ashling had not known how to dance, yet in the pale woman's arms she knew. They swept around the earthen floor like fleshly visitors to a dream, and as they danced they spoke.

'My lover rejoices at your presence,' said the woman.

Ashling looked around for a glimpse of anyone who could possibly be this woman's mate. 'Who is … ?'

'Breathe in,' said the woman.

Ashling breathed in the heavy scent of bittersweet decay.

'That', said the woman, 'is my lover.'

They danced on, silently weaving between the faded ghosts, who revelled in the dance. As they swept past her, they plied her with food and strange, bitter drinks. She took all she could, ecstatic, abandoned, ravished by strangeness in this sweet, dark world. Then, abruptly, the music ended and the dance stopped.

'You must decide now. Would you go or stay?'

The question seemed ridiculous. Of course Ashling wanted to stay. She said so.

'Very well. Eat, then. A gift, from the garden.'

In the delicate, long-boned hand lay twelve ruby pomegranate seeds. Pomegranate seeds … she was remembering something. Something she had read too long ago … Yes! She knew!

'I … don't know if I should …'

The woman's face darkened behind the mask. To Ashling it was all too perceptible. 'You come into our world, accept our hospitality, partake of our food and our wine, you dance with Persephone and breathe Hades into your mortal lungs, you ask to be allowed to stay, and now you dare say you doubt?'

Ashling did not feel wronged. She felt in her every atom the justice of Persephone's words. Yet she was still afraid.

Persephone touched her shoulder, not roughly but with authority. 'You know what you truly wish,' she said.

Ashling thought about her life.

A half-nude man sits on the edge of the bed. 'It's not that,' he says. 'Last night was really special to me too, but I just can't handle a relationship right now. Look, I'll ring you, okay?'

A young girl with unkempt brown hair – now somewhat tamed – trips a plain girl in the corridor. The girl looks up, and her injured eyes are just like her own.

Ashling presses forward in torn dress and muddy boots. Never again, she tells herself. No more.

Steeling herself, she took a breath and ate. She felt the room smile, warmly and hazily. She felt Persephone's smile, surreal, super-real, behind her white-bone mask. 'Now,' said Ashling, 'why don't you show me your face?'

Persephone smiled again. 'Give a man a mask and he will tell you the truth,' she said.

'Not me,' Ashling murmured. 'Never again. No more.'

CUT HER DOWN

See me, you world hungry for harvest.
I stand up.
I show myself.
I say, '*I* am John Barleycorn.'
I will stand alone in the green field,
Baked by sun, chilled by frost, swept by sweeping rain.
Bind my hands together.
Bind my feet.
Crown me with poppies, red berries,
Poison-berries and poppies with a shadowy bloom.
The pollen will fall on me,
Light on my eyelashes
And make me golden.
Now I am ripe, and heavy, doubled with burden:
So cut me down,
Cut me down,
That again, green and lovely,
I may grow and touch the sun.

SIREN

I like to sing when I am lonely. I like the way it carries across the water, like a message in a bottle smashed. It flies with the sea-foam and idles pleasantly in the calm. I like to think that it holds some of what I used to be, and peeks into caves and down into the wrecks of ships, as I did once. Once, when hope was boundless, I did not think to imagine that, all the long years of my life, I would be alone. I was a sensual explorer then, with a head full of warm beaches and strong, willing men. One day, a sturdy-legged sea captain would take my hand and lead me on to the shore, or else dive with me and live as my husband beneath the waves. Or perhaps a handsome negro crewman, or a fair and starry-eyed cabin boy, young as myself.

So I waited, and one day the ship came. It was raining heavily that day, and I was singing my little wordless tune across the water. She came as though buoyed by my own breath. She was a sight to behold. A massive, nude, armless woman, red-lipped and flushed, dark hair blowing half across her face but not hiding the great, grey eyes, led the vessel forward. And oh! She was beautiful. So beautiful that I might have snaked myself round the painted, wooden form and forgotten my loneliness. But then I saw the Captain. He was steering strongly against the driving rain, and I marvelled that he could hold control over this great woman who was so welcoming yet so inscrutable. He had no beard, though his long hair suggested he had been a long time at sea, yet he did not look boyish or effeminate. He was every inch a man as he turned the ship and blinked the rain out of his eyes. And then he looked at me.

Lost in the delirious fleshing-out of my fantasy, I carried on singing, and his eyes would not leave mine. The ship approached my rock, just like I had dreamed, but if I had taken my eyes from those of the Captain I would have noticed that he was no longer steering it so. It was caught in the current. How it haunted me, that first time. As the ship drew near I held out my arms – child, thoughtless child – and smiled. What happened next must have happened in quick succession, or even all at once, but memory has painted it as a hideously drawn-out agony. First, I realised that he was no longer in control of the vessel, which was approaching a treacherous rock. I gasped, and as I stopped singing, his expression turned from enchantment to confusion to disgust and fear. I did not know how long his crewmates had been shouting and pulling at the wheel, but suddenly I perceived them. In his last moments he looked at me with revulsion, and his lips mouthed the words, 'Christ, what is it?' Then, with a ghastly crunch, the ship-woman rammed into the rock. She splintered, her lush painted skin cracking to reveal the wooden heart. She no longer looked alive. When at last I found the Captain among the wreckage and the bleeding men, his eyes were as dead as hers.

You might call it a grim little garden, my sweet bed of drowned men among the seaweed. But I am numb to the horror of it now. Besides, the end justifies the means. One day my Captain will come to me, my husband, for ever. And he will not give up when he hits the water, or look at me like a monster. Many ship-women have come and gone. Most are nude, and if they are more than a torso they have a body like me. Men with legs desire women with tails; but they fear us. They die in the water rather than be with us. Someday, one of them will be man enough to live.

O DARKNESS, TAKE MY MIND

O Darkness, take my mind.
It will spiral up like a black bird,
Here and there shedding a feather
That flashes gold in the light
Of a candle that is not there.
It will swoop through the roof
And up into the night-time
To spread out across the stars.
O Darkness, take my mind.

O Quiet, take my voice.
In the daytime, this singer-bard,
This artist of words,
Is like a great painter
Who scribbles stick-men on post-its
All day.
I abuse the many-coloured words
With unmemorable, bleating talk.
But now all that floats into the world
Is the simple eloquence of my breath:
In and out.
In and out.
O Quiet, take my voice.

O Night-time, take me.
I am afloat on a river of stars.
The breath of a thousand sleepers fills my sails.

Sail me, sail me, to the mysterious end of the day,
Where the water spills over and people whisper of monsters.
And down I will fall,
Cradle and all,
To float on the darkest sea.
O Night-time, take me.

INVITATION TO A DANCE

I once courted twins. Each lovelier than the other. One pursued me like a courtesan; the other evaded me like a hunted doe. One served me; the other threw down the gauntlet. One was Aphrodite, the other the Sphinx. One bore a blown rose, the other a sword like a thorn. And they were both the same. Gods, how to put a name to such beauty? But that is what I had to do. Buried at the centre of each was a sparkling kernel of name. A cold, hard diamond tarnished by disuse, abandoned by memory. Such was my quest: to feel beneath the layers of these wondrous creatures, cold or yielding, and reach for that blackened diamond, that heartstone, at their core.

It was a wonderful, frightening upheaval of souls, something akin to a dance, or a battle. It was a movement of entwining and entangling, of hiding, holding and weeping both sad and joyful tears. These women were not simple. Not easy. One day they would rip out a great part of me with their claws. The next they would replace it with something miraculous that I did not understand. Only then would I realise that, with a few exceptions that I would have to rescue and heal, the parts they ripped away were neither good nor right. You may wonder how I could possibly be man enough for these two, my angel, my succubus. The answer is simple, though perhaps unpalatable. I am a shapeshifter. That is to say, I have two shapes between which I may change at will. One is very like a man. The other rather more like a dog.[1]

---

[1] I would ask anyone reading this not to imagine that my human form was the better, the more civilised. To call someone a 'cur' by

This reminds me that I have not yet described in full our endlessly strange and intricate, painful and lovely dance. For as my twins and I revolved around one another, so bright twin turned about dark twin turned about bright twin, and dog-man waltzed with man-dog. It was as complex and epic a web of orbits as that of the spheres. But its music was not the melodic tinkling of angelic choirs. It was the sound you hear when you put your ear to the ground.

These magical women were the constant Goddess herself. They were fixed in their dancing orbit, dancing it with the fierce dedication of concert virtuosos. But I am not a virtuoso. I am an amateur: a faltering lover with only occasional flashes of brilliance. And I get distracted. Let me tell you now about the Game of Distractions. It is a fun game, and 'fun' is the best word for it. 'Fun' is an easy word to say, though a little dark, like 'fen' and 'gun'. And so is the game: easy, though riddled with dark undertones. It started off innocently, like everything does. A doll here, so pretty, with blue closing eyes, a rhine-stoned, pink cellophane-covered stick of rock there. Just little toys and sweets and treats. But once it becomes an obsession …

The first day the Goblin Market came into town, I came across it accidentally. I just walked through a veil of rain and there it was, hung with its dusky fruits, feverish with life. Now I don't claim to know much of life, but I do know well enough how to read. That is why I cannot claim innocence. I have read Rossetti. I have learnt of the sweet, pale child who turns paler, sickens and wastes for the want of goblin fruits. She rests her locks of fading gold on her sister's breast, and they kiss, and kiss. I found the tale not cautionary but desperately erotic. It

way of an insult is to belittle the noble creature that guards the gates of the Underworld, that walks by the side of our Grandmother and Witch Queen Hecate and that joins the Fairy Folk on the Wild Hunt at Halloween. Reading *Steppenwolf*, I wanted to eat the arauca-ria plant.

made me crave goblin fruits and pale virgins. So when at last I came across the Goblin Market it seemed that I owed it to myself to take a break from the dance of love (had you forgotten? were you distracted?) and enjoy a hungry look at those lush wares.

The goblins, in their moss greens, in their violets, looked at me heavy-lidded and knowing. With inviting smiles and musical speech they evoked the honeyed succulence of their fruits. I could not make out the words, but I seemed to hear it on the hot, wet wind: just a little; just a little; just a look; just a smell; just a brush of firm or yielding flesh against the lips; just a drop of juice on the tongue; just one; just one.

So I walked a little farther into the Market, farther from my twin loves and my quest, and for the first time I tasted goblin fruit. I shall tell you two things about that fruit. First, that it was deliriously, gorgeously sweet, like lychees, honey and elderflower, like the debauched mango, the silken-skinned peach, like women's fragrant flesh and hothouse blooms. The second thing, inevitable, irrefutable, was that it held no satisfaction at all. Pleasure, yes – thick, blood-hot, indulgent pleasure – but no satisfaction. No relief. No release. Just more want, and more, and more.

I ran back to my twins with the taste of addiction still on my tongue. It was delicious and it sickened me. I was useless for desire and shame. I danced with them, eagerly, madly, but I had forgotten all the steps. I had, in fact, forgotten entirely the point of the dance. I danced to compare their snakelike bodies with the warm skin of goblin fruit. I forgot to wonder over their ineffable names. So they would not dance anymore. In their stillness they were terrifying. They were cold as queens carved in granite. I loved them more than ever. For shame, I lay my head upon their cold laps and wept. We did not kiss and kiss. It was not erotic. In my darkest despair, in my unrighteous anger, my thoughts turned to goblin fruits.

It is a myth, you know, that the Market disappears and

leaves us to pine away. No, it waits for us, lies in wait for us, to feed us until we die. No silver? No coin? Never mind, they trust that you will pay someday. Such was my life, for too long. It's my dog nature, of course – my happy, careless, indulgent dog nature. But that dog can also hold on to things tenaciously. It began to dance again, when the man-flesh was weakened beyond dancing. It danced well, with flair the man did not possess. And can you imagine? It caught their names. My blown rose, my bloodied thorn: it felt for their heartstones and held them! And to celebrate, it went to the Market and forgot. I, I the man, was nearly dead. I was seeing skulls and rotting fruits before my eyes. And every time my dog nature danced it expertly plucked the names from my loves and poisoned me before I could learn them. So it was that the man in me died. The hardier dog nature gave up on me, trained itself to ignore the deadly voice of addiction and finally whispered to the twin goddesses their secret names.

And so he lives to this day, the dog-headed man and his two loves. They have beautiful children.

Love stories sometimes are very, very strange.

FLOWER

Draw my petals around me,
A touch of velvet or sueded closeness
Enveloping in the glowing pink
Of autumn sunshine through closed eyes.
There I'll hide,
Folded in shadow and scent,
Dusky, honeyed,
As one unborn floats in space
Within the mother.
Yes.
Cover me.
Place me in a flower, in a fragile prison.

A woman made of tears,
Of shuddering equilibrium,
Of unrealised weeping and surprise wrapped in promise,
Touched her wrists with fragrance,
Vulnerable over the hot living pulse,
A prelude to a warm song of blood.
She hides in an aura of blossoms,
Hides in the forest of her hair.
No monsters will see me through this veil.
There is no harsh light and no horror.
In this flower I'll stay,
Cradling a rootless moment that exists
In my mind.

ABSINTHE

It is 1899, and John Taylor Markiss's fingertips emit sparks of fire. He likes Blake for his romantic lunacy and his 'Proverbs of Hell'. Mostly, though, he despises those English Romantics with their flowered talk of shepherds and nightingales. That is how he came to be in Paris. Paris, where wealthy men's courtesans are as well known as their wives, and even the centime whores look like penny arcade Sarah Bernhardts. Where poetry and revolution are irresistibly en vogue and the world awaits (he is so sure) a messiah like him. The sun does not need to shine here, now, on the cusp of a new century in the centre of the world. Even in the dull fog at dusk the cafés give a soft, coloured glow: strings of paper lanterns all along the Champs-Élysées.

Here, Markiss feels comfort and delicious fear in equal measure. The Paris nights envelop him in the fumes of strange alcohol and good tobacco. The ghostlike mist encircles him, embracing him. It offers up a sharp, soft, smoky kiss. Yet there is one insistent element that teases him. What is that strange, complex, medicinal scent rising through the smoke and the red wine? Some drink, he imagines, but no common one. One moment, he is sure he smells nothing but anise. The next, the dangerous scent of unknown herbs grows up around it, creeping and choking like ivy. He covers his face, but the scent remains. Maybe it was never there at all. Maybe it is all in his mind. He imagines his own skull, creeping with weeds. Then he steps into a café and there it is: the source of the green-white haze that fills his head.

A group of young bohémiens are talking, animatedly and scathingly, of Rimbaud: 'Il était génie en enfance, mais en âge si bourgeois.' Suddenly, they stop, with the hushed reverence of the church. A waiter approaches them, holding a tray. On the tray, among several antique-looking artefacts (bell-shaped glasses, slotted spoons, carafes and sugar bowls), there stands a bottle. It is green, like a jewel, and labelled 'Absinthe'. The hushed bohémiens begin to pour molten emeralds into their dusty glasses. The scent drifts behind his eyelids. Markiss is bewitched.

*

John Taylor Markiss sits in his dark appartement, his dusty jewel beside him. The ritual conjures the spell, makes the potion fit for poetic madness. First, he uncorks the bottle. He has long discovered that la Fée Verte does not have functioning wings. She creeps out of the bottle, her body an invisible mist, as beautiful and maddening a mistress as Poetry herself. He knows, now, what her body is composed of. Yes, there is anise, but also Florence fennel and, ruling them all with imperious hand, grand wormwood.

He pours a dose of absinthe into the bulbous measure at the base of the glass. He balances a tarnished silver spoon on the rim and places a lump of sugar upon it. He lifts the carafe, so cold it steams, and tilts it very slightly. The first drop of ice water seems to disappear. The second barely dents the sugar. With the third the dent gapes a little, and the fourth causes a droplet of white syrup to hang suspended from the spoon. A fifth drop, and it falls to swirl into the clear green below. And so it goes. Markiss lets droplet after droplet fall. The sugar collapses, and the absinthe slowly turns a cloudy, pearlescent white. The elixir prepared, he takes his first sip. It tastes like anise, and bitter herbs, and clear-headed genius. The Green Faery's arms close about him, her hair falls about his face and he begins to imagine words.

*

Markiss eats as little as possible. He finds it desperately prosaic. Gourmands are so rarely good poets, he says. His life is spent, in the main, drinking, writing and burning what he has written. Nothing, nothing is quite right. Nothing rings true. He is sure the muse – that which the Irish-born in London called, prettily, Leanan Sidhe and which he knows to be la Fée Verte – has chosen him. Yet even now, after so many weeks of her embrace, when she opens her mouth it is only to breathe her bittersweet breath upon him; never to talk. He vows to eat even less, to stop his whoring and his casual affairs and to dedicate his life entirely to poetry and its bottled muse.

*

It has been raining again. The sky in paroxysms of sorrow. It batters the windows like the ghost-child's grasping hand: let me in, let me in. But Markiss does not fear the smashing of the window, or little Cathy's grip, cold as death. He knows the colour of the halo of protection: it is palest white-green and fragrant as incense. He now eats only two small portions of bread moistened with water in a day. He is listening. He is listening. Out of the bottle rises la Fée Verte, and he braces himself for her blessing and her whorish caress. But he does not feel her wonderful, ghastly embrace as he normally does. Instead, she comes close, pressing her lips to his mind, and she speaks.

She speaks marvellous words: revelatory syllables and sounds of such exquisite beauty and meaning as to ravish with loveliness. Then she says, 'Lock it up, John Taylor Markiss. Lock it up tight in the box in your mind, never to be written

21

until I send you the sign.' And with that she is gone.

Markiss rejoices. At last he is the poet he dreamed of being. And one day, at the sign of the muse of art, he will write all he has learnt and change the world – for nothing can be the same after knowing those words. Every day now is the same, except that every day she embellishes the divine verse and tells him, 'Soon, soon now, sooner than yesterday.' His fingers itch to write, but he is faithful to his lover and queen who crawls out of the absinthe bottle. He will not write until he is given the sign.

*

It is midnight on the Champs-Élysées. Markiss feels omnipotent. The absinthe is coursing through his veins, making the world tilt to a more attractive angle. Suddenly, he is hit by a tilting wall, and then an undulating pavement. Spreadeagled on the ground, Markiss regards his surroundings. The pavement seems strangely vast, and beside him, squat, dirty, but inviting, lies a stub of white chalk. Then an ice-wind whistles through him, and it smells like sugared green herbs and says, 'Now! Now!' Raising a grateful hand to the wind, Markiss takes up the chalk and begins to write. He weeps as he writes, and shivers – he imagines from the cold, though that seems very far away. As he writes it begins to rain: thin, stinging rain that seeks out the neck beneath the collar. He does not care. All he sees is the next word, the next divine syllable. He writes and he writes, and though he does not look back he can well imagine the vast pavement covered in poetry, white upon the steely grey. Slowly Markiss becomes aware of leaving his body. He can see himself scrawling below, but the chalk has gone. His fingers have been worn bloody on the rough pavement. The last few lines are written in blood.

*

John Smith was found frozen to death on the Champs-Élysées. It took some time to discover his identity, since he had few acquaintances in Paris and, when he had spoken to others, had for reasons unknown used an alias. He had evidently collapsed drunk in the rain. When they found him he was lying on his front, his hand frozen in the attitude of writing. He may have been chalking on the pavement, for some chalk dust was found mixing with the rainwater near his body. Of course his last words – if any – were washed away by the rain. No one saw him in his last hours, but one witness – though she insisted she was half asleep and may have been dreaming – thought she saw a woman, dressed in the manner of a courtesan, walking away from Smith's dead body. Her skin seemed a pale emerald green. Perhaps, after all, it was just the light.

PERFECT BALANCE

Perfect balance
Plucked me from garish reality:
Placed me on the line
From which (here and only here)
All I can see are leaf-gold shafts of autumn sunlight.

Perfect balance.
The fibre of the rope
On the soles of my feet
Cuts only to the truth.
If I bleed, it is right that I should bleed.
A drop wells and falls,
Tawny as Proserpine's fruit.
It dyes the ground for a moment,
Bright against soft grey,
Then sinks and is gone.
In its place blooms Asphodel.

Perfect balance
Is enthroned in smiles and tears.
As long as it lasts, it lasts.
When it ends, I fall.
In my place blooms Asphodel.

SOULS

I lived with a girl in college who wouldn't let me photograph her because she believed the camera might trap a fragment of her soul. The wickedest thing I ever did was to invite her to my exhibition. I never told her the theme. Just led her by one thin, pale, freckled hand to the room that I half-knew might drive her mad. The title of the collection was 'Fragments'. The collection itself: shot after shot, flaming colour on the stark white wall, of stolen shards of her soul. Here the haphazard red brushstroke of her hair, taken from behind. There a sharp profile, bent over a coffee cup. Next to that, a distance shot – naturally, there were a lot of those – of my lover looking up at a grey sky. In those days, I dealt in shock. Thought that shock was the upstart brother of art. God knows I learnt my lesson.

I might as well have offered her a room full of windows on to Hell. Her eyes grew frighteningly wide, an expanse of sickly white drowning the green. For a few seconds her mouth stretched open. No sound. Just ugly silence. Then she turned to me and I saw that her terror had wilted to pathetic hurt. I had stabbed her somewhere vulnerable, somewhere cheap and too easy, and here I was holding the bloody knife and expecting her to praise my cleverness. At that moment, perversely, I itched to photograph her. I'm sorry, Wendy, wherever you are. I should never have done the thing that I did. Only now do I see what made it so easy to do without guilt: you see, I never really believed you had a soul to steal.

*

Fifteen years later, I was no longer actively stealing souls. I was still taking pictures. I made great heavy coffee-table books. A series, with boundless potential: *In England* by Richard Tye. *Cafés in England. Sea Lore in England. Christmas in England. Childhood in England.* And one year, *Halloween.* It was the night itself and I'd surprised no one with the pictures I'd collected. Hosts of little skeletons and witches huddled in twilight doorways; teenage girls done up like cats draining a wine bottle on a car park wall; goths kissing in a graveyard; New Age types lighting candles to the beloved dead. Clichés all, but a nicely shot cliché sells a thousand art books. One of the New Agers – they called themselves witches – tipped me off about Glastonbury.

Over a post-ritual cup of coffee he told me the story. Every culture has its Lord or Lady of the Dead. Ours is Gwyn ap Nudd, the White Son of Night, and he lives beneath Glastonbury Tor. Right, I thought. It was a pretty idea and I was charmed. Every year at Halloween he rises up with all the hordes of the Otherworld to gather lost souls. With spirits, witches, faeries and demons he flies on the Wild Hunt, plucking wandering ghosts and tortured glimmers to fill his Land of the Dead: behind the veil, beneath the hill.

Maybe it was the atmosphere – coffee fumes and lingering incense – but all at once I was taken with the idea that I might drive to Glastonbury that night. Why not? It wasn't far, and it was Halloween there as much as anywhere else. More, if this man was to be believed. If not, good on him: he'd spun a good yarn and I'd bought it. Not that there was a Death God living under Glastonbury. I doubted that even that guy – who could with all seriousness address and offer wine to a photo of his dead grandmother – believed it with a whole heart. But there might be more of these self-styled witches in the fabled Isle of Avalon who knew the myth and could re-enact it for my lens.

Two hours later I was wandering vaguely towards the Tor. Colder and darker here than in the city. Otherwise, not much different. You got me, witch-man. On the other hand, a mist was falling, thick and white, appropriately atmospheric. Maybe a shot of the Tor through the mist, with an explanation of the myth of Gwyn ap Nudd?

Stop. Wait.

What?

In the time it had taken to formulate that thought, the fog had grown so thick I couldn't see. Everything was white. White like the walls in that exhibition room long ago. White like Wendy's eyes. My mind was shorting out, unable to conceive of so much white. And then it was gone. All that was there was the Tor. I turned back. The mist hung weirdly in space. I'd come through it. So, here was the Tor. Except … no. No tower. I'd gone wrong somewhere in the mist. But I couldn't go back into it. Anything but that.

Funny how, when someone appears over the brow of a hill, it can look like they're emerging from the hill's belly. Someone was coming that way now. He was pale, moon-pale, and riding a paperwhite horse. The figure was followed by another, and another, all on horseback, winding down the steep hillside. There were dogs, too, their baying voices echoing in the empty night, their pale shapes flanking the horses. I saw all this through the camera's eye. This was a beautiful kind of madness and I wanted to keep it, fix it. By the time I realised I was in danger, it was too late.

The horses thundered towards me. I cried out, flashing the camera like a flare, but instead of stopping or trampling me they missed me by a clear metre and began to circle, hooting, whooping, their eyes feral.

'First of the night,' said the leader of the procession, his voice clear and rich.

I looked at the pale man and my frightened mind tried to call his whiteness a death pallor. But no. He was very much alive, white not like dead flesh but like a fat moon in a country-

27

dark sky. His eyes held all that midnight in them, including a frosting of stars. He wasn't normal. None of it was normal. Even the horses, pure white from a distance, had blood-red ears.

Sharp hands, suddenly under my arms, lifted me and threw me on to the back of a horse. I scrambled to right myself before I fell. Then we were gone – howling through the night, impossibly fast. The speed, the fear, became a kind of cool, clear trance. I wondered, through the swiftness of flight – Was it flight? Were the horse's hooves touching the ground? Were we skirting the stars? – I wondered, what has happened to me? Have I been picked up by a bunch of crazies in fancy dress? Mythological re-enactors? More witches? Have I got exactly what I hoped for? Or more? No. No, no, no. There is no Gwyn ap Nudd, no Land of the Dead, no Wild Hunt for souls. Don't worry about that. You're just …

… in big trouble. Or mad.

The landscape below was no longer like Glastonbury. At least the horse was clearly real, its hair wiry, its flesh warm as blood. And if it was a real horse, then these must be real people. It was OK. My brain didn't have to collapse in helpless panic. I comforted myself with the assurance that they might not be supernatural beings. They might just want to kill me.

'Where are we?' I called into the wind.

'Avalon.' I could only see the back of the leader's head, his black hair lifted by the passing air.

'This isn't Glastonbury,' I said. Did he think I was stupid?

'No, it's Avalon, and you *are* stupid. But not for long.'

I clung to the horse's neck, smelling the mundane farmyard scent of him and the biting ozone of autumn midnight as the wind whipped around me. The stars blazed past, growing comets' tails, stretching out on either side of me. The sky was everywhere, underneath me as well as above. I remembered something the witches had said in their Halloween rite: 'As above, so below.' The illusion of flight (for it was an illusion, surely) was so wondrous, and I so terrified of falling the imaginary distance to my very real death, that I didn't even register the fact that the leader of these wild dogs had apparently read my mind.

Abruptly my horse swooped down. I screamed, clutched at air, falling faster than gravity. Then, quite as abruptly, the horse was under me again, and another man sat behind me. The ride resumed as though nothing had happened. I had the feeling of having experienced a glaring continuity error in my reality. The man behind me felt real. He patted my back jovially, laughing fit to burst.

'Thank God,' he said, his voice delirious with relief. 'They were late for me. But you can't choose when they pick you up. Just wander and hope.' He sighed. 'How long was it for you?'

'… How long?'

'Fifty-seven years for me. To the day!'

I rested my forehead against the horse's mane and squeezed my eyes shut. For the first time I considered the possibility that I might be dreaming. I quickly dismissed the theory. The wind, the condensation wetting my face and my hair, the muscular body and coarse hair of the horse, my heart pounding fast in my ears – this was visceral.

'Yes, I'm in the Halloween Club,' the man behind me went on. I strained my head around and saw a tired-but-jaunty-looking man with slightly receding hair. He looked to be in his early forties. 'Got on the wrong end of a nasty trick. Kids put a Roman candle through the window. That'll teach me to sleep through trick or treat.'

'Um. What?'

'They burned my house down.' He smiled, cheerfully.

I closed my eyes again and shook my head. I was so accustomed now to the speed of flight that it seemed churlish not to engage in Dadaist small talk with the friendly stranger whose house had apparently been torched before he was born.

'You look pretty happy about it,' I ventured.

'Well, it *was* fifty-seven years ago.'

I looked back at him again, my grip on the horse's neck loosening for an instant. In that instant I slid sideways and my stomach lurched as I grabbed a handful of coarse hair. The horse shook its head and snorted.

'No,' I said, 'Nothing happened to you fifty-seven years ago.'

He put a hand kindly on my arm. 'You must be newly dead,' he said.

I laughed.

'It's a very scary time. A very strange time. I'm sorry. It's easy to forget when it's been so long. When did you die?'

Enough. 'I didn't! And neither did you. Look at you! You're fine. You're not ninety years old and you haven't been burned to death. You're not a ghost or a zombie. You're just ... normal! You're fine!'

'Denial,' he said sadly. 'Watch that. You'll have a hard time.'

I looked at him once more, then turned to face front. The leader still rode impassively before me.

'Hey!' I shouted. 'You! Whoever ever you are!'

'You know who I am.' The leader's voice rose effortlessly over the whipping wind as though on a separate plane.

'I know who you're gonna say you are,' I said, no longer bothering to shout. How absurd my clinging to the processes and attitudes of normality seems now, looking back. Like a green actor sticking hopelessly to the script as the theatre burns around him. 'Look,' I went on, 'just let me off, OK? I don't want any trouble.'

'Who ever *wants* any trouble?' he reasoned. 'Just calm down and accept it. You're dead. You're here. You'll be in the Otherworld soon.'

Gwyn ap Nudd.

Childish fear welled up like tears. 'I'm not dead!' I cried. 'I never died! I'm not meant to be here! I'm not!'

Gwyn stopped short. The wind stopped with him. The

world fell deathly silent as though at the flick of a switch. I felt the eyes of the other riders upon me, pools of suspicious black.

'If you're not dead', Gwyn asked, 'then why are you taking up space on a horse?'

In that instant the horse was gone from under me again. For a moment I anticipated its return. It never came, and I fell. I heard the crack of my bones on the ground at the foot of Glastonbury Tor, but saw neither mist nor faerie host.

That was how I joined the Halloween Club. That was why *Halloween in England* sold so well, and why I never saw a penny of the money. An unfortunate way to discover that you have a soul. I still think that, somehow, it was all an apt punishment for Wendy.

I've been wandering for eight years.

It's lonely.

I'm tired.

Roll on the Wild Hunt

MY GRAVE

I place a garland on my grave,
The flowers red as blood.
There is mist this night, and a haze of rain,
And it is true country dark.
Among the smoky ghosts I weave,
Rain droplets on my hair and face,
And reach the grave where I must place
A tribute to myself.
Sorrow! I am to die.
My grave is a gaudy shrine:
Skulls and flowers,
Incense and sequins,
All the crazy colours of death.
And at its head sits the Baron,
Smiling that unholy, holy smile
And guarding the doorway
I am unready to cross.
I weep for my own death,
Put my effects in order.
I hide from the reaper at the door.
My death fills me with horror only once
But not again.
Don't you ever cry for me.
For when I finally find my grave,
Decked out, with the Baron at its head,
I will drink and toast my death
And cry joy for the fullness of my life.

TRAMPS AND THIEVES

They sit on the brink of perception, so that you think you have only dreamed them. Marco remembered them some mornings, hazy in his mind like anaemic hallucinations. They were clustered around a junk fire. They smelled like night-time and black coffee. But they weren't real, Marco was sure of that. They were too genuine to be real. Falsehood, lies, pretend – that was real life. He had known it at the age of twelve. Father was always more comfortable in his role than Mother was. Father played the computer dogsbody by day and the loving hubbie and pa by night, and never seemed to mind. Mother went through the motions but looked like a spooked wild animal in a cage. She was a bad actress. No awards for that performance. When she cried, the greasepaint smeared and you could almost glimpse a person underneath. That was when Marco loved her most.

The crying and the sadness: at least those were real. Poignancy and darkness tugged at Marco's soul. He longed for companionship in the dark, for a bond of blood that was vital and ecstatic and frank and true. At seventeen, he thought he found it. They looked like him: pale, gothic, too intense. They had read the same books as him, so he thought they wanted what he wanted. It was an exciting world they inhabited – at least, it seemed that way at first. They studied 'magyck', which they spelled that way to mark it out from inferior, rabbit-out-of-a-hat 'magic'. They wore dark velvet clothes and dyed their hair black. And they had a secret that drew secret smiles from their dark red lips. They said, we need to be sure we can trust you.

They said, be true to us for a year and a day. Then, they would tell him. A year and a day. The magyck books said that was significant, but they never said why. During that time, Marco was slavishly devoted to his attractive new friends. He aspired to being half as charismatic as those men. He aspired to bedding such elegant women. He was hooked on their mystique and their mystery.

After a year one of the girls, flushing beneath her pale make-up, pressed a folded letter into his trembling hand. The letter was on stiff paper, with a red wax seal in the form of a pentagram. He broke the seal. It was an invitation. The party would be at the house of Petyr, one of their number. They all took exotic names like that. The paper felt good, cool in Marco's hand. He prepared for the party. That Sunday, with a huge, orange harvest moon outside the window, Marco teased his black hair into its most dashingly eccentric style and dressed himself in his black velvet suit. He looked in the mirror. In the moonlight he felt that he looked otherworldly. He felt like one of them.

A twist of smoke twined out of the door as it opened. It smelled like dope and incense. The beautiful girl who had given him the invitation beckoned him in. Her name was Lamia, and every now and then he thought he could sense nervous excitement brimming beneath her easy gothic languor. Tonight it was more pronounced, barely concealed by her corseted crushed velvet gown. Indeed, the general atmosphere was strangely high-pitched despite the haze. Gradually the sounds of Joy Division were muted and a hush fell on the party. Petyr approached him. He was dressed in a tail coat and top hat, his long black hair hanging low beneath it.

'Marco,' he said warmly, 'you have been loyal to us for a year and a day. You have shown yourself worthy. And so we have seen fit to initiate you.'

Marco remained silent. Little nervous gasps and smothered giggles came from the throng.

'You see, Marco,' Petyr went on, 'we are a coven of vampires.'

Here Marco laughed, but quickly stopped himself. 'I'm sorry,' he mumbled, 'but – you know – that's impossible. I mean it's … you're interesting and everything, but you're definitely human.'

Petyr's face darkened. 'Vampirism is not a matter of race,' he said. 'It's a way of life – an ancient way of life. Of course we're human. The myths built up because people feared the magyckal power of the vampires. We've read certain … texts. We've recreated the Old Way. Blood is power. If you want, that power can be yours too.'

Marco's eyes were wide. 'How?' he asked. 'What is … what does the initiation involve?'

Petyr's face relaxed into a smile. If Marco had not been entirely taken by Petyr's coaxing words, he might have noticed the hungry, edgy excitement mounting in the room. Petyr squeezed Marco's shoulder.

'We will feed off you. Just a little at a time – it's more symbolic than anything. And only until we feel that the time is right for you to progress to the second degree. At the second degree you can begin to feed. What do you say?'

Marco looked into the brotherly face of Petyr. 'Show me,' he said.

Petyr drew his lips back in a grimace to reveal pointed canines.

'Those aren't real!' Marco exclaimed, a little frightened.

Petyr smiled. 'No, they're not real, but they work. Internet. Easy enough to find, but damned expensive. They're razor sharp and they channel the blood. Let me show you.'

Marco tensed as Petyr approached him, but the pale, long-fingered hand on the back of his neck was comforting and somehow sensual. When Petyr's plum-painted lips touched his neck and the sharp canines pierced his skin, Marco let his head fall back and leaned into it as though into an embrace. He would never have imagined that something so odd, so perverse and wrong, could be so erotic. Petyr's fingers were playing with the hair on the nape of his neck. His lips were moving on Marco's neck, leaving plum-coloured lipstick marks, and his tongue lapped at the blood that he drew from the tiny puncture wounds. When he stopped and drew back, his lips were red with blood. Marco had a few dazed seconds to admire the sight before he lost consciousness.

Marco awoke on Petyr's chaise longue as Lamia was placing a flannel in some iced water beside him. It had evidently been on his forehead, for the cold and wet had roused him. In the course of the night, every member of the coven fed on him and he passed out three more times. The last time was when he discovered that Lamia, unable to afford vampire canines, had to use a razor. Fortunately, she stopped short of slashing his throat and contented herself with sucking on his forefinger. And despite everything he loved them all. They got under his skin, as it were, to the vital pulse beneath.

But weeks passed. The tenderness, the eroticism, dried up before his supply of ready blood did. He was invited to all the parties, but he no longer participated. Not really. Not actively. He sat on the rug in the middle of the room, where the bong or the shisha pipe might have been. Some of the coven no longer remembered to interact with him – apart from his abused wrists or the tender hollows of his elbows. Some treated him fondly, like a pet. Lamia lowered her pretty eyes and apologised again and again as she cut him with a razor. 'In time, in time, in time,' they murmured whenever he mentioned the second degree. But time was running out. I'll be dead by then, he thought. I'll be dead.

In his bloodless lethargy Marco found that his eyes were opened to the reality of his situation. He saw his pale companions for what they were. No coven at all, but a group of rich

36

goth kids looking for a hit. They had read, perhaps, a little Crowley and a lot of Anne Rice. And maybe at first they had believed the pretence they sold him. But that was over now, smothered in the freaky, thrilling party haze. Now he was trapped in another lie. He hated it. But if normality was a lie, and rebellion and deliberate weirdness were a lie, what else was there for him?

*

There is always something else. They sit on the brink of perception, so that you think you have only dreamed them.

*

He fell out of the door of the ground-floor flat. It was a misty or perhaps a smoky night that mingled with the salt seaside air, and that added to his confusion. As he dropped from his knees to the ground he saw them once again, fleetingly, out of the corner of his eye. They were beneath the pier. Their silhouettes stood black against the gold of a dancing fire. Colours of jet and amber. Then his eyes filled with night and he slept like one dead.

When Marco came to, he was no longer numb. For the first time in months he felt completely awake and alive. He knew, for instance, that one side of him was cold and gritty, while the other side was blasted with heat. He could see, at an odd angle, an alien landscape, menaced by dark hills. But no ... no ... He was lying, half on his front and half on one side, gazing at the sandy ground centimetres from his shining eye. The hills, they were ... what? Boots. Brown boots. He hauled himself up, imagining himself a tangled marionette, then recoiled. Right into the fire. Marco righted himself then fell again, not burnt but shocked, into bare brown arms. He spun round. Dark, dark coffee-bean eyes stared at him, wide and challenging. She was rather thin, dressed in flowered rags that might have been a dress at one time, or a bedsheet. Tarnished silvery bangles hung about her thin wrists, and she was compellingly lovely. She was also intense to the point of frightening. A large, rough hand landed heavily on Marco's shoulder, and he turned once more to look at the character who had scared him into the fire.

The man seemed to be mostly beard, and the parts that weren't beard were rags and jewels. Teeth nestled in a barely visible mouth, chequered grey and black and gold. Marco thought the man was smiling, but it was hard to tell. Then the man caught Marco's hand in his. Sea-worn and dirty, with black and bitten fingernails, the hand was adorned with rings that looked like they could have been real gold. It swamped Marco's pale and tapered fingers like a father's hand around a child's. Finally, he spoke. 'You look lost,' he said.

Marco bit his lip and glanced awkwardly at the motley gathering around him. He was unsure whether to pull his hand away or whether to leave it there too long would be the more unwise. 'I'm not lost,' he said. 'I live just … just over there …' but as he gestured vaguely towards the fog-touched lanes he realised that he did not know. Had they teased the information from his sleeping mind? Or had it been killed by months of degradation of the flesh? Or was the truth that everything had slipped into the whirlpool of his life, leaving him, finally, homeless?

'Who are you?' murmured Marco.

'Tramps and thieves,' answered the man. 'Some loons, some loners. Perhaps some of us see things. Tamora says she does, don't you, Tamora?' He was looking at the lovely girl, who looked more than anything like a storybook drawing of a Gypsy.

Tamora looked up with the air of a startled bird, nodded once and went back to studying the fire. Its tendrils reflected hypnotically in her dark eyes. Marco decided not to quibble over whether the man meant that Tamora saw things in a lunatic or a prophetic sense.

'And what about you?' he asked.

The tramp smiled beneath his beard, or so Marco guessed. 'I'm the King, so I don't require any other talents. Good thing, too.'

King. Right. Why not? Marco was under a pier at night with a band of street folks, wearing his pale make-up and black velvet suit, with hair awry and puncture wounds on his neck and wrists. Somehow life had strayed so far from normal that the idea of a Tramp King seemed quite reasonable.

'Should I call you … "Your Highness"? "Your Majesty"? "Sir"?'

The Tramp King laughed, and a chatter, as of seabirds, came from the assembled crowd. 'You can call me Frank, because that's my name.' He made it sound both mystical and stupid.

Marco flushed, feeling ridiculously affected. 'Frank,' he acknowledged. 'Hello.'

'Hello,' chorused the strange crowd in uncertain unison, some jovial, some wary. For the first time, Marco was able to look at each one. Frank's description – tramps and thieves, some loons, some loners – seemed accurate. One tiny woman in a huge, worn fur coat held in her arms a small, dirty-faced child of indeterminate gender. One snakelike man with several hoop earrings in his left ear periodically sniffed the air and shot angry glances at nothing all around him. A long-haired boy no older than Marco and in fairly normal clothes smiled shyly from under his fringe. A woman in a large hat and a dress that looked like it had once been orange waved rather too enthusiastically. A small group of children ignored Marco entirely, engrossed in their game of marbles. A black man with hair dyed pale blond and violet eyes stared impassively. And then there was lovely Tamora.

She caught at his hand as Frank had done, and hers was tiny in comparison. She placed a scuffed deck of cards in his hand.

'Take,' she said, as though she could not speak much English.

'Thanks,' said Marco, captivated by her eyes.

Tamora tutted. 'Take!' she repeated. 'Three!'

Marco's mind processed the request. 'You want me to take three cards?'

She tutted again. 'Three,' she said again.

Without looking he chose three cards and she snatched them back and held them close to her face. Then she laughed – a short, barking laugh – and threw them to the floor. The others looked at her expectantly. 'He stays,' she said, and the crowd went back to their strange poses. The woman in the once-orange dress, Marco noticed, was still waving. That he had been in the line of fire had been purely coincidental. The long-haired boy had sat down to play marbles with the little ones, though he was easily fifteen and probably even older.

'Hang on,' said Marco. 'What do you mean "He stays"? Oh, the oracle has spoken and Marco stays on the streets! Well I don't want to gloat, but I have a home to be getting to, so … bye.'

But Marco no longer knew his home. The seaside lanes were a spiralling labyrinth of darkness, and every turn took him back to these strange few, these destitute, oddly comforting Nightkind. That was the word Marco coined for them. They were the Nightkind because they seemed formed from living night. When eventually he gave up looking for his home, he found he didn't want it anymore. He sat down with the long-haired boy, who put his arm around his shoulders and gave him a marble. Tamora passed him a paper cup of steaming black coffee. And somehow it was right. Nobody talked much, and Marco noticed that when he was with the Nightkind the daytime never came. Never did 'real life' – life full of lies and pretence – come to find him. All that existed was of the quiet hours of the night: the fire that warmed them and the distant fires of the stars, the coffee and gentle companionship, and the blue-black sea tiding on the darkened shore.

'One day we'll all go back into the sea,' Frank murmured one night. The others nodded and murmured assent, and Marco looked at him questioningly. Frank seemed to smile. 'Our kind, we always go back into the sea sooner or later. If we stayed around too long, people would start to get suspicious. You can live a little more than a human life, but not too much more. I'm a hundred and fifty. Tamora there is a little more than that. We grow too old. Besides, the night would stagnate if it were populated with the same folks for ever. New folks will come from the sea, fresh and young folks, to live in the night-time and breathe out life to the moon and stars. You're too young to remember how beautiful the nights were when we were children. We made them so fine … but we're all old now. So old.'

So that was what they were. Marco had guessed that they were just poor and half-crazy, and himself half-crazy with them. They had not boasted like Petyr's 'coven'. They had kept a simple silence, not a mysterious one. And now the truth came out, it all seemed so humble.

'What's in the sea?' asked Marco.

Frank laughed. 'What's in the sea? The sea's in the sea! Ah, I can see you're thinking of us all dancing with friendly fish, aren't you? You're seeing Tamora as a little mermaid, yes? Well the sea's not a cartoon. Or an aquarium. It's the sea. It's the Great Mother. It's the deepest deep. And that's where we're going.'

For a while they were all silent again. Then Marco turned suddenly back to Frank and, holding him by the shoulders, said, 'Take me with you!'

'Out of the question. You're a young man. Your place is in the Dayworld. You're just visiting. No. Out of the question.'

Tamora, who had been crouching by the fire, jumped up and looked at Frank indignantly. She passed him three cards

41

and gestured towards the dark sea. 'Just because the cards accepted him, doesn't mean the sea will. Not necessarily. He can't risk it. And he's too young to know what he wants. Best just let him be.'

'No,' said Marco, 'I *can* risk it. I want to. This is the first real thing I've ever found. Let me.'

Frank put a hand on his shoulder. 'If you're not meant to be with us, I can't promise that there'll be anything for you after you go into the sea. What I mean is, if you were to drown … Well, I just can't tell you you'll meet up with your loved ones in Heaven. What do I know about it? I would hope, for your sake, that your soul would go somewhere better, but … I can't in good conscience say everything will be all right in the end.'

A tear ran down Marco's cheek, made hot by the blast of the fire. 'Thank you,' he said. 'Thank you for not saying everything will be all right.'

*

In the end, they all go back to the sea. They take torches lit from the fire to light their way in the deepest deep. They step into the water and it is not cold. It takes them beneath its waves like a mother. What they see in the deepest deep is not to be told. But it is good and true.

Later that night, if you are awake at witching time, you may see the night turn newer and more lovely. The moon seems paler against the black. The stars burn with a newer light, and the clouds part so that they can be seen. The footprints from the sea to the place beneath the pier are washed away in the tide. And perhaps sometimes, when you're confused or seeing unusually clearly, you will see them on the brink of your perception.

You will think that you have only dreamed them.

THE EMBRACE OF
NEPHTHYS

A time between time,
A world between worlds,
No time,
No place,
And on and on the sand stretched,
Silver-black as moondust,
And it was no sand,
No sky,
No sea.
And we stood,
And we never stood,
And still we stand,
And if you can find
That world-not-world,
That time-not-time,
You will see our footprints there,
Filling with water,
For ever.
And perhaps, our shadows,
Still stretched across the sand,
Remembering the night we stood for eternity
In the embrace of Nephthys.

THE TIDAL WAVE

The King of the Sea told me once that I was sea-foam in human form. My skin is peach coloured: neither pale nor olive nor chocolate nor ebony. There is a soft covering of downy hair on my arms. Here and there are little brown moles. I hardly have the look of a mermaid. I looked like a mermaid that day, though. The day he told me, I was stretched out on a cliff ledge in Boscastle. I had hitched my skirt up around my waist and put my bare feet into a little, sparkling pool on the narrow ledge. So it did not seem so strange.

He rose up out of the blue-white water where it beat against a far cliff. He whispered to me – I swear! And he left the taste of saltwater upon my lips. And oh, I can remember all I saw there, though the memory resides in my blood and not in my mind. I remember the boy with the sad step on that far cliff, the boy who always laughed but never smiled, who would climb and climb until no one could follow him. I remember the grinning rock, the one we called Old Man Gardner, and the little geysers by him. And then, when the Sea King sank back into himself, I remember the touch of my friend, my sister, calling me back to the World. She was reading me a poem by her own hand.

So this happened. And my life went on for many days and nights, with mundanity and mediocrity and small fears. And I tried to find a niche for myself in the World and in Grown-Up-Life. I was a fairly pretty woman on the outside, a world, a whirlpool, a demonic, silly, useless, wonderful, inhospitable changeling child on the inside. And, of course, I loved it and hated it. Who was this girl, this child that my sensible self had to tend? Strange child. Luck child. Seventh daughter of a seventh daughter. Cowrie shell bobbing on an open sea.

I returned to Cornwall many years later, not to bright Maytime Boscastle, but to cold February on the shores of Tintagel. So cold. The pale sky shivered with the beating black wings of crows. They are the masters of the Castle now. And I stood on the stones and shells, close as I dared to the surf. And then it came for me. It came, the wave, the great wave that somehow I had always known would come.

At first, a tremble on the surface of the water.

Gooseflesh on my skin.

Then a stirring of the foam.

A stirring of my blood.

Then a great swell of the bleak water – an arc many times my size – and it was bleak no more. For, as I watched, the great arc turned to a swell of pure crystal blue. I saw gilded and green and rainbow fish dancing in the wave. I saw long-limbed women with sea-foam skin. I saw strong horses stamping their hooves on the blue water. And then it covered me, and I saw through crystal-water eyes. I saw the muted, grey-beige shore and all its quiet, hidden life. I saw the people I knew, all cold hands and windswept hair, greatcoats and wellington boots. I saw the white winter sky. And I knew.

I stepped out of the wave then, and down it sank as if it had never been there. But I, I never looked through my sad old eyes again. This is something I have never told anybody, because it never really happened. Yet here it is, scratched in black ink on pale paper. This tale is imagined, but the stones and shells and cliffs of it remain. Old Man Gardner still leers at the swelling waves, the seasons still roll from Maytime to winter and on and on, and the crows still fill the skies at Tintagel.

I AM ALL INK INSIDE

I am all ink inside,
Pressing myself against the page.
I am all ink and dark stars,
All breath of salt spray seashores at night,
All wet siren rocks
And sea music.

HEALING

'Where do you come from,
Daughter of Breath and Air?'
Murmured the endlessly sewing Mother,
Hunched in the murky shadows.
The thread was wound all round her hands
And about her head.
Blue thread,
Grey in the grey darkness.

The daughter spoke
Like a warm breeze at Beltane.
'Look upon me!' she laughed,
And her body was a mist of water droplets
Blushing with rainbows in the sun.
'I come from the taste of pear juice on the tongue.
I come from the scent of incense in summer.
I come from naked skin in the sunshine.
I come from the breathless lustful glance!'
And she danced and danced.

The Mother sewed endlessly.
She sewed silly, ugly things together.
She closed her eyes so that she could not see how ugly they
were.

'And where do you come from, Mater Lachrymosa?'
Shimmered the Daughter in tones of pure joy.

'I come from bondage to devils,' she said.
'I come from sexual repulsion.
I come from guilt.
I cry and cry and the pain never goes.
I never cry when I think I'm being watched.
I bite my fist rather than make a sound.
I bite my tongue until it bleeds.'

*

Sit in a dark room.
Light candles – the candles are important.
Watch them flicker in the faces
Of your kindly gods.
Remember in your anguish
That these plaster statues
And picture cards
Hold gods inside them.
So do the candles.
So does the sky outside,
And your fractured mind,
And your broken heart,
And your tired body.
Then dance! Dance!
Erzulie dances in you.
Baron Samedi is in the graveyard.
La Sirène purifies your bath.
Papa Legba is at the door with a rattle and a grin.
Oya smites your enemies.
Hail to the gods in you!
Cry a tempest,
And break through the clouds with a smile of sunshine.
That's the way to heal.

'Come into me, Mater Lachrymosa,'
Cried the Daughter,
And she, in her ecstasy, was weeping.
'Come into me and dissolve into summer rain.'
'I can't.
People will miss me.
I must sew things together.'
But she went anyway.
And the daughter hurt as they merged,
Worse than she had ever hurt before.
And then the sadness was gone.
Funny how these things can happen
All of a sudden
If you let them.

BRIDEY

Spring came early that year, because She deemed it should be so. It was January still, but the watery sky beamed with a reckless blue. Midges rolled on the warm air currents. Some trees burst into pale blossom, which flushed dusky pink when other, more sober trees looked disapprovingly at their extravagance. Ana could feel the turn. At these times when the seasons turned she felt more intensely alive. Her eyes seemed to open wider. Her skin felt the texture of her clothes. She was aware of her tongue in her mouth and her hair falling over her shoulders, and of the vast expansiveness of her own mind.

Today, she sat up in bed in the late hours of the morning, cradling a cup of coffee in her hands and gazing out of the window. The coffee was good, strong and dark with a bitter chocolate scent. It conjured images of the visit to Cornwall at Beltane, when they had walked the tropical trail in the Eden Project and seen the colourful history of the cocoa bean. She laughed to herself. She recalled the shape the milk had made as it poured into the deep black of the coffee. It had been a three-armed cross, which spiralled in the darkness before it merged with the black. Brighid. Spring was here for sure.

Ana was a nut-brown brunette with black coffee eyes and a searching expression. She was the product of love (her parents) and bullying (her peers). She was fiercely loving, constantly awed and resolutely strange. For Ana, everything was magic. She rode the yearly cycles. She honoured the gods. She tied ribbons to trees. She tore her blouse and stained her skirt picking blackberries. She walked in fountains. Yes, she was strange. And she was happy.

Ana put on her lace gloves and stepped out into the air. It was warm, with a shiver of rain on the breeze and a sprinkling of undisturbed dew underfoot. She didn't know where she was headed. She just needed to be out in this miraculous spring. The suburb of Thorn was airy and relatively green. Two magpies squabbled on a rotting tree stump. More birds started from a tree, frightened by a noiseless noise. Ana walked down the park road. As she walked she sang:

Oh I am come to the low countrie: ochon, ochon, ochrie!
Without a penny in my purse to buy a meal to me ...

The warmth of the air and the hum of the traffic and the gentle patter of the rain sang with her.

The Forest Park was alive. Snarling hawthorns (some already bedecked in blossom) and wise elders and holly trees great as oaks smothered the iron fences and concrete paths. The fishponds were green and opaque, bordered by huge, flat, foreign leaves: bayous from another time and place among the British trees. Ana loved the wildness. It was here that she picked the blackberries and elderberries and sloes, marigolds and yarrow, broad flat mushrooms for frying and little wicked ones for flying.

Ana watched a little blackbird scratch around at the bottom of a blossoming may-bush. Blackbirds were her favourite. Smart yellow beaks and bright black eyes. They did not gossip or fight. They seemed always focused, always on a mission. The scratching blackbird turned to her, blinked and called. She stared. She had tried before to follow blackbirds, convinced that they were calling to her. Each time it had ended with the bird flying away or disappearing into undergrowth too dense for her to follow. The bird fluttered a little, as though troubled by an itch, righted itself and stared at her once more. She started after it.

Soon enough, the blackbird disappeared through a hole in the hawthorn. Ana reached out and touched the may. The branches were coarse and thorny, but the soft blossoms left a sheen of silk on her fingers like a welcome. Hands held palm-outwards in front of her, she walked forward. The hawthorn seemed almost to part for her. Yes, the thorns scratched her and tore at her clothes, but what had been impossibly dense was now allowing passage. Ana closed her eyes and felt the blossoms touch her eyelids, anointing them with their spring scent.

When she opened her eyes she was no longer in the Park. Or else the Park had taken on a shimmering super-reality. Dull brown-grey had turned May-green. Stooped, arthritic crone-trees had straightened until they looked like fresh-faced maid-ens, tossing green locks and shaking blossom bracelets on lithe arms. Some trees were tied with coloured ribbons, red rags, paper, equal-armed crosses of pale yellow reed, rainbow threads and locks of hair. Where her memory of the Park's geography told her there should have been a swamp-like fishpond, there was now a circular fountain. The water was clear, but left stains of rusty red. And sitting in the fountain was a woman.

The woman looked nothing like Ana, and Ana had never seen the woman before, and the woman was Ana's mother. Ana had never laid eyes on anything like this woman, and rec-ognised everything about her. Tears welled in her eyes. Walking towards the fountain, she reached out to the woman. 'Lady,' she whispered, 'Great One, Goddess, Brighid …'

Brighid took her hands and looked at her with a familiar ex-pression. 'Call me Mother,' she said.

Ana sat down in the water in front of the Goddess, and cried. She had not cried so since she was a very small child. She felt very small now. Great sobs shook her body, and she did not know why but she knew it was good, and right, and some-how wonderful. She held the Mother's hands tightly, and her tears fell on Brighid's dress. After some time Ana could cry no more, though she shook and coughed for a while longer. Finally she looked up at Brighid, who looked so large compared with her, and the Goddess smiled down with a mother's indulgent mock disapproval. She scooped up clear water with two hands and washed Ana's face.

The Lady began to talk. 'Where I go, snowdrops and daffodils and many candles follow my step. Where I walk is the purifying and the transforming flame. Where I put my feet, healing water wells up out of the ground. This is a world of no winter. This is a world of health with no blight, of rhyme and beauty and the eternal embrace of the Mother. I ask you, would you like to stay here?'

Ana looked around her and took the Mother's hands again. 'Lady, Mother, I am so honoured, so happy, to be allowed to see you like this. I can't describe how happy. And it's so beautiful here. Of course it's more beautiful than the old, twisted Forest Park. It's far more beautiful than Thorn, the estates and roads, and the supermarket on the corner. But before too long I'll want … I'll need … to go back. Here it's beautiful but it's almost … too beautiful. Too special, too exciting, too comfortable, all the time. It's an honour to be your child but here I'd just be … *a* child. I need to be an adult now. I need to create things of my own. Is that … is that all right?'

Brighid laughed and kissed Ana's forehead. 'All right? Yes, all right in every way. No child of mine stays tied to her mother's apron strings all her life. Never lose your wonder. Enjoy the Earth that you have been given. You are ready now for your greatest work. I am satisfied of that.'

'But what, what will this great work be? I can never finish anything. Will I write that novel? Will I persevere with my painting?'

Brighid shook her head. She leaned down to Ana and whispered:

Call her Bridey.

Ana's eyes filled with tears again as she understood. When she wiped them away, the green had faded to brown once more. The red fountain was an emerald-green pond. The trees were arched and bare. But wait: there was still one offering tied to the tree. The embroidered cloth said 'Bridey'. Ana took it, replacing it with a ribbon from her hair, then turned and walked back through the hawthorn bush. The blackbird, still sitting there as though on guard, nodded at her then flew away. Ana walked back down the overgrown concrete path, one hand on her flat, young girl's belly, and wondered.

A STRING OF LIGHTS

Wind on the hill:
Clasped hands
Anchoring paper dolls.

*

In this night mirror
You see not yourself
But fish, and stars.

*

His breast
Is full of fire
And we dance.

*

The blue wood
After tears:
Let us storm the church.

*

Every night,
Her breath
And love, and relief, like a wave, like a wave.

*

This string of lights,
So sudden,
Snatches life from time.

www.awenpublications.co.uk

Also from Awen Publications:

The Long Woman
Kevan Manwaring

An antiquarian's widow discovers her husband's lost journals and sets out on a journey of remembrance across 1920s England and France, retracing his steps in search of healing and independence. Along alignments of place and memory she meets mystic Dion Fortune, ley-line pioneer Alfred Watkins, and a Sir Arthur Conan Doyle obsessed with the Cottingley Fairies. From Glastonbury to Carnac, she visits the ancient sites that obsessed her husband and, tested by both earthly and unearthly forces, she discovers a power within herself.

'A beautiful book, filled with the quiet of dawn, and the first cool breaths of new life, it reveals how the poignance of real humanity is ever sprinkled with magic.' *Emma Restall Orr*

Fiction ISBN 978-1-906900-44-1 £9.99
The Windsmith Elegy Volume 1

Iona
Mary Palmer

What do you do when you are torn apart by your 'selves'? The pilgrim poet, rebel Mordec and tweedy Aelia set sail for Iona – a thin place, an island on the edge. It's a journey between worlds, back to the roots of their culture. On the Height of Storm they relive a Viking massacre, at Port of the Coracle encounter vipers. They meet Morrighan, a blood-thirsty goddess, and Abbot Dominic with his concubine nuns. There are omens, chants, curses … During her stay Mordec learns that words can heal or destroy, and the poet writes her way out of darkness. A powerful story, celebrating a journey to wholeness, from an accomplished poet.

Poetry ISBN 978-0-9546137-8-5 £6.99

Exotic Excursions
Anthony Nanson

In these stories Anthony Nanson charts the territory between travel writing and magic realism to confront the exotic and the enigmatic. Here are epiphanies of solitude, twilight and initiation. A lover's true self unveiled by a mountain mist ... a memory of the lost land in the western sea ... a traveller's surrender to the allure of ancient gods ... a quest for primeval beings on the edge of extinction. In transcending the line between the written and the spoken word, between the familiar and the unfamiliar, between the actual and the imagined, these tales send sparks across the gap of desire.

Fiction/Travel ISBN 987-0-9546137-7-8 £7.99

The Firekeeper's Daughter
Karola Renard

From the vastness of Stone Age Siberia to a minefield in today's Angola, from the black beaches of Iceland to the African savannah and a Jewish-German cemetery, Karola Renard tells thirteen mythic stories of initiation featuring twenty-first-century kelpies, sirens, and holy fools, a river of tears and a girl who dances on fire, a maiden shaman of ice, a witch in a secret garden, Queen Guinevere's mirror, and a woman who swallows the moon. The red thread running through them all is a deep faith in life and the need to find truth and meaning even in the greatest of ordeals.

Fiction ISBN 978-1-906900-46-5 £9.99

The Fifth Quarter
Richard Selby

The Fifth Quarter is Romney Marsh, as defined by the Revd Richard Harris Barham in *The Ingoldsby Legends*: 'The World, according to the best geographers, is divided into Europe, Asia, Africa, America and Romney Marsh.' It is a place apart, almost another world. This collection of stories and poems explores its ancient and modern landscapes, wonders at its past, and reflects upon its present. Richard Selby has known Romney Marsh all his life. His writing reflects the uniqueness of The Marsh through prose, poetry, and written versions of stories he performs as a storyteller.

Fiction/Poetry ISBN 978-0-9546137-9-2 £9.99